MY FIRST
I Can Read Book®

Loose Tooth

story by Lola M. Schaefer
pictures by Sylvie Wickstrom

HarperCollins*Publishers*

Loose Tooth
Text copyright © 2004 by Lola M. Schaefer
Illustrations copyright © 2004 by Sylvie Wickstrom
Printed in the U.S.A. All rights reserved.
www.harperchildrens.com

Library of Congress Cataloging-in-Publication Data
Schaefer, Lola M.
Loose tooth / by Lola M. Schaefer ; pictures by Sylvie Wickstrom.—1st ed.
p.   cm. — (My first I can read book)
Summary: A young child experiences a loose tooth for the first time and eagerly
waits for it to come out.
ISBN 0-06-052776-5 — ISBN 0-06-052777-3 (lib. bdg.)
[1. Teeth—Fiction. 2. Stories in rhyme.] I. Wickstrom, Sylvie, ill. II. Title.
III. Series.
PZ8.3.S289Lo 2004
[E]—dc21
2003006322

1 2 3 4 5 6 7 8 9 10
❖
First Edition

For Maddie
—L.S.

To Sosha,
who just lost another tooth
—S.W.

It's loose.

It's loose.

My tooth is loose!

I can see it.

I can feel it.

I can pull it.

I can push it.

But it won't come out!

It's loose.

It's loose.

My tooth is loose!

I wiggled it for Brother.

I wiggled it for Mom.

I wiggled it for Sister,

and my good friend Tom.

But it won't come out!

It's loose.

It's loose.

19

My tooth is loose!

I just ate an apple.

I bit a hard nut.

I chewed a long carrot.

And—guess what?

My tooth is loose,

loose,

loose.

But it won't come out!

Brother says, "Pull it!"

Sister says, "Wait."

Dad says, "Let's see."

Mom says, "Too late!"

My tooth came out

with NO help from me.

Now there's a hole
where my tooth
used to be!